BROWN VOODOO
MESSIAH

BROWN VOODOO MESSIAH

A Microfiction LP

RAN WALKER

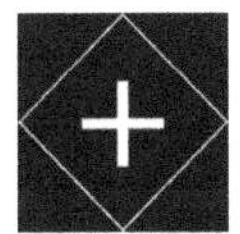

BLACK + SQUARE, LLC

ISBN: 978-1-961753-24-2 (Paperback)

ISBN: 978-1-961753-25-9 (Ebook)

First Edition
10 9 8 7 6 5 4 3 2

Black + Square, LLC
Hampton, VA

CONTENTS

AUTHOR'S NOTE

Like many people who were privy to the full career of D'Angelo—from thumping "Lady" in the Jeep to nodding my head to "Another Life"—I was saddened by the all-to-soon loss of this music legend. I found myself listening to each of his albums, from beginning to end, reminiscing on my own life and how his music served as a soundtrack for many moments, and I knew I had to do something. I had to channel this feeling of loss into something that might celebrate our brother and welcome others to do the same.

This is my first time attempting a microfiction structure like this. The aim was to simulate the feeling of a double album (or as they call them nowadays "deluxe versions") by putting together a series of 100-word stories that drew off of D'Angelo's songs. While the stories/prose poems can stand alone, if you are a fan of his music, you will find more than a few Easter eggs.

I hope that you find some comfort in this collection and that our brother rests in power evermore.

—Ran Walker
10-15-25

In Memory of Michael Eugene Archer,
a/k/a
D'Angelo

A KWANSABA FOR D'ANGELO

take me home to the old porch
swing where big mama gave us sweet
tea but told us too much would
rot our teeth and we laughed voices
rich like chords on a fender rhodes
high hat ticking with crickets at sunset
our souls dancing into brown sugar dreams

I make music because it's the way I express
myself. I make it for people to feel.

— D'ANGELO

REST IN POWER

SIDE A
VINYL 1

BROWN SUGAR

Rick loved on Mary Jane like Spider Man, but neither of them have the love I have for Brown Sugar, a love like neighborhood friends who grew up to be lovers and make real hip hop, my mind elevated like astrodynamics where I rap with Sagan, Tyson, and Hawking, Einstein ring on her finger like we're hopping the cosmic broom and flexin' on galaxies, and she rocks me like I'm her baby—not infant—her Luther and TLC "baby, baby, baby" and I suckle at her nipple and pull the cloudy soul from her like Venkman, Spengler, Stantz, and Zeddemore.

CANDY-COATED THOUGHTS THAT DRIFT THROUGH MY SLEEP

He remembers the possibilities, the what-ifs, pondering what could have been if things had happened differently, but un-forgiving fate was their antagonist, and now they are left to absorb D'Angelo's crooning like a shot of cognac. He remembers Donald Glover's quest to find the brown voodoo messiah in the restroom of an Atlanta gas station, and maybe in that maze he could find his way back to her, through thick, soulful falsetto and memories fresh like popped tennis ball cans. Maybe he could reach further than the lyric, than the abstract—theoretical—across the infinite, to lie with her again.

WHY AM I WEARIN'
HANDCUFFS?

The song comes on the radio while I am driving, and I immediately know the chorus will be instrumental. Frankly, I'm a bit surprised there is even a radio version—and it's not just the song's title. You rarely hear a song where the protagonist kills his wife and best friend because he caught them cheating, but here we are.

I fill in for D'Angelo's crooning on the chorus, saying what he can't say, doing my best to say it the way he does, all the while shaking my head.

It's a catchy song.

Don't judge me.

Shit. Damn. Motherfucker.

I BE KISSIN' WHEN I'M
KISSIN' WHAT I'M MISSIN'

FOR ELLE

I love you like a metaphor.

I love you like H.E.R.

I love you like Brown Sugar.

I love you like pink cookies in a plastic bag getting crushed by buildings.

I love you like the song I have been replaying on repeat for the last half hour as I write this for you.

I love you like the first kiss, the last kiss, and every kiss in between.

I love you like words I can't even pronounce but use just because I want to try to capture this feeling for you on the page.

I love you.

THE CHERRY IN MY CHOCOLATE-COVERED DREAMS

There are few things he is sure of, but she is one of them, though she has no idea that a version of her tip-toes through the tulips of his dreams from haunting ukulele to Fender Rhodes, bliss blossoming on brainstems like roses dripping rain from a Saturday afternoon. He wouldn't dare tell her the truth of his feelings, lest she twist them like mall pretzels doused with fake butter and sprinkled in half carat salt rocks. No, he will cherish her only in his dreams, where love is requited and the soundtrack of D'Angelo carries him on into infinity.

I CAN TELL THEY'RE LOOKING AT US

*A**h, ooh ah ooh ah.*

Can you hear it? They're singing it at the end. Wait, you can hear it much better on the London live recording.

Yep, that part. That's my shit!

Yeah, I know they're not words, but make no mistake about it. They are definitely lyrics.

And that bass? Yep, that's Raphael.

Oh, you like him? He's on another track in this collection, but we'll save that for later.

I'm hungry for food trucks—excuse me, food stands. You?

Sure, there's no shame in my game. You're with me. They can look all they want.

My lady.

SIDE B
VINYL 2

VOODOO

uest is drunk on the drums, and Pino is leaning so far back from the beat, his bass skipping like the child trying to avoid all the hopscotch numbers at once, and D'Angelo's fingers rest above the keyboard, waiting for the spirit to hit him so he can dive into that syncopation like Louganis and splash around, wetting the floor with perspiration, his voice trying to channel the pain of the moment Gina said she couldn't do it anymore, where he understands his wife is the music, and he has decided he will do her until death do us part.

DRUMMER'S DRUMMIN'
RIGHT

We walk through the door, swag blue whale heavy, nuts dragging across the floor, and we grab the instruments on stage and rip the roof off like Preacher Boy, Quest building hypnotic beats into towers like the ones we used to build from Legos in kindergarten. And the asses swing and heads nod because we didn't come to play with y'all, but we'll play *for* y'all, and you'll take this groove home with you, pushing it between sweaty hips and thighs—that kick hitting you right. Rim shot strikes like a sonic boom, and y'all sleep, bodies still like caskets.

SECRET ROOMS IN THE
MANSIONS OF MY MIND

He once wrote a story based off a D'Angelo lyric. That poetry prompted his imagination, and he created a story where a man painted pictures of a muse who appeared to him in his dreams, only to find that she existed in real life.

It's funny how art begets art, he thinks, not fully appreciating that he would one day write an entire project inspired by more than a single song, that he would sit with the canon of lyrics and melodies, grooves and incantations, and from these, fashion varied pieces, crafting something new, something seeking to reverberate with soul.

SOLE CONTROLLER IN
CONTROL OF ME

The most beautiful of sunny days cannot dry up the storms you have rained upon my doorstep, this water flooding around, between, and through me, as I anchor myself like a battle ship in the chiseled concrete that was once my foundation. You tried to rip it clean, but my prayers are cement, and the water you attempted to drown me in, mixed with Earth, helped me to build one stronger, so I am not particularly concerned with how you take this, your feelings no longer chains around my throat, but, honestly, I ain't got nothing to do with you.

[UNTITLED]

He tries to speak, but his words collapse into accelerating breaths, staccato, syncopated supplications, begging for this moment to be infinite—even expanding like the universe—and she swallows his body whole, her limbs holding on to him for dear life, as the swell begins to build within her, like the crescendoing of a trumpet, its blare coming so hard that her face catches fire with longing, the two of them linked—coupled—like trains without brakes, clinging to the rails like gravity will soon depart, and all either can think to ask the other is, "How does it feel?"

SHE'S ALWAYS IN MY HAIR

After the homecoming coronation, she invites him back to her one-bedroom apartment off-campus. There, she lights the candles across her bedroom, like Nola Darling preparing her temple for sacrifice, and she lays him down slowly, undressing him and affixing his wrists to the posts of her bed with silk scarves.

She has decided she will not make love to him tonight, though, but she will have him wanting her in a way his rational brain will never be able to process, and she will live in his dreams, dancing in the ecstasy of his thoughts, just beyond his fragile grasp.

SIDE A
VINYL 3

BLACK MESSIAH

His knuckles are not scarred, scraped, stiff, blackened, callused, calcified, or swollen, but that does not mean they do not still make a fist, one that is just as Black, just as strong, just as powerful, and he will lift it alongside the other fists, shades the gamut of dawn till dusk, as their imaginary torches release real flames that stretch back over generations like John Bigger's sketch of Harriet Tubman, and, in lock-step, he will move, one step at a time, toward the future for which his ancestors have steadily been marching, heads unbowed, arms weary but never wavering.

I'M IN REALLY LOVE
WITH YOU

Even now as your body welcomes me, your skin tinged in moonlight, door locked to avoid interruptions, I am filled with the same love that came through the fingertips that once caressed your hips, the motions of your younger self, giving me you, seeking to glimpse my hungry soul, understanding that it would never abate, and here we are: your legs wrapped around me as if remembering some beautiful moment in our history, our present, our future, and loving you feels natural, so real, so beautiful and infinite, and I know, without question, that I'm in really love with you.

PREACHER'S KID, PART 1

I can feel the praise rolling off the sanctuary walls, shouts to our savior as natural to the ear as my brother poking me in my side and whispering about Ms. Beatrice's legs, admiring them with his own praise, but I am focused on the organ keys just off the pulpit, forlorn, missing me like I'm missing her. Pops winds down, touches his ear, my cue to get get back to her, slide beneath her, purrs moaning and mixing with the others, the walls bouncing us back and forth, all heads bowed, as I lift my head to the heavens.

I'M A GOOD MAN, AND I WORK HARD ON MY NIGHT JOB

She'd asked him why she should be with him and not someone else. This is how she liked to force him to show his desire for her. He knew it was just a game, but he wondered why she felt the need to toy with their relationship like this. He would remind her that he was more than just good loving and money, that he was a good man, that he wanted to be the one in whose arms she found comfort, solace. She would smile and kiss him.

He just wished she'd find a better way to do this.

THE STONE MASON

You loved me when my sound was not perfect, when my body was not perfect, when I couldn't keep on schedule or make it all come together. Your love was both the chisel and mallet that you wielded skillfully like Michelangelo to reveal what truly lay beneath. Your loving touch smoothed my rough places, and your full lips kissed mine, while you whispered that the world would love what you loved, though I know you weren't ready to share me—just yet. Still, we know music cannot be contained, nor can love, and eventually you'll have to let me go.

THE SOULQUARIANS

Oh, to be a fly on the wall of Amir "Questlove" Thompson's crib, watching legends revolving and evolving through the doors like some kind of Neo-soul carousel, music so loud the police can hum the grooves on street corner shifts where the vibes get leaked ahead of the drops, and fans claim sightings of D'Angelo and Erykah, Common and Mos, Bilal and Musiq, and someone even claimed to have seen Dilla, and the center of the earth was taking form around their block, and it seemed like it would never end, lest someone try to photograph and write about it.

SIDE B
VINYL 4

CORNROWS

He sits two steps beneath her on the stoop, her brown thighs brushing his shoulders, her fingers oiling his scalp and separating his hair with a rat tail comb, like Moses planting his staff into the Red Sea, waves stretching to the end of each strand. She is like a spider weaving an intricate web, his hair catching moans of the ancestors, rhythms from the fields. He licks his lips and smiles, and in this moment he is her king, her lover, her brown voodoo messiah, and the paths she creates along his scalp lead the way to her heart.

PASTORIOUS

Their love is a fretless bass guitar, where the frets have been slowly and sloppily shaved or cut or burned or chopped off, one at a time, over years and even longer years, while the musician continues to play, adjusting and adjusting until nothing remains except Jaco's long, callused fingers holding its neck, careful not to choke or suffocate the melodies, and they know they will not remain together, but the art they cre-ated—*oh the art!*—is too beautiful, too painful, to infinite to ignore, so they try once more and once more and once more and once more….

21

PREACHER'S KID, PART 2

His voice is thick like molasses, too thick to drag a biscuit through, but sweet enough to put on top of anything, be it biscuit or bacon or a slab of country ham, thick like Grandma's arms, covered in flour and faded grease pops, thick like the girl who likes to smile at him after Sunday school, while she talks with her girls and swears she never let him finger her behind the chapel after vacation bible school, thick like being Black in the South, sprouting in the shade of Dixie flags, managing to see God in everything around him.

U WILL KNOW

Every superhero has an origin story, a lyric that unites him to the canon, to the other superheroes who were once young and full of wonder. It all starts with a dream, this Black boy imagining the infinite possibilities, discovering that he possesses a power few others have. Then he will learn how to use it—then use it for good— and if we are lucky, this superhero will be known for his deeds, for the lives he has saved, for the gifts he has shared with others. This angel will become the messenger for a generation united in soul.

ELECTRIC LADY

Jimi's spirit is in every corner of the studio, Betty Jean and Black Beauty still whispering their incantations, hypnotizing everyone who sets foot in the room. Michael and Amir will converse with the ghosts of yesterday in this place, creating a sanctuary for Pino, Russell, Roy, Premiere, Charlie, and everyone who will convene for this seance. Here, they will build, demolish, and rebuild walls of sound, of soul, over and over until they abandon the idea of perfection in favor of greatness. Now their spirits will inhabit this studio, along with Jimi's, and others will feel them when they come.

MAGIC WAX

He bought the record from a vinyl store in Alphabet City because of the image on its cover. Listening to it for the first time, he quickly realized that every time he dropped the needle a different song by the artist played, as if the entirety of the artist's discography was somehow magically captured on both sides of the vinyl. He tried to record it, but the playback was always silent.

One night, he fell asleep as the record played. When he awoke, the record was gone—but his reflection in the turntable shimmered, offering something he'd never heard before.

❀ 25 ❀

I WANT YOU FOREVER

I love you so much.

I can say these words over and over for nearly ten minutes, but you will never understand how deeply I mean them. These words travel through all space and time and resurrect themselves as soon as they slip off my tongue and die at the edges of my lips. They are my mantra and soundtrack, my gift from Jeymes, my testimony. They are the summation of my melodies, my sounds, and my voice. They are the arc of my life's creativity, and if it be the will of the Almighty, my final words to you.

ACKNOWLEDGMENTS

Special thanks to Elle, Torrey, Sabin, and Rel.

ABOUT THE AUTHOR

IN 100 WORDS

Ran Walker (he/him) is the author of over 40 books. His short stories, flash fiction, microfiction, and poetry have appeared in a variety of anthologies and journals.

He is the winner of the Indie Author Project's National Indie Author of the Year Award, the Black Caucus of the American Library Association Best Fiction Ebook Award, the Virginia Indie Author Project Award for Adult Fiction, and the Blind Corner Afrofuturism Microfiction Contest. Ran is an Associate Professor of English and Creative Writing at Hampton University and teaches with Writer's Digest University. He lives in Virginia with his wife and daughter.

The Golden Book: A 50-Year Marriage Told In 50-Word Stories

Keep It 100: 100-Word Stories

A Burst of Gray: A Novel In 100-Word Stories

The Library of Afro Curiosities: 100-Word Stories

Black Marker: A Novel in 100-Word Stories

GloKat and the Art of Timing: A Novel in 100-Word Stories

A Different Kind of Christmas Story: A Carol in 100-Word Stories

Spaceships Don't Come Equipped with Rearview Mirrors: 50-Word Stories

This Is Not a Poem/Story: 100-Word Stories

Parts of Speech: 100-Word Stories

Four Suits: A Deck of 100-Word Stories

Oʻahu: Prose Poems

Apollo's Toy Box

Gods Among Men

One Hundred Ways: A Handbook for Writing 100-Word Stories

Sneaker Marauders: Poems (with Van G. Garrett)

The Night Before the End of the World

Fragments of the Afroverse: 100-Word Stories

Deux: A 50 x 50 Micro Novella

The Seven Wonders of Stevie: Kwansabas

Trevor's Room: A 100 x 100 Micro Novel

Brown Voodoo Messiah: A Microfiction LP